This Walker book
belongs to:

_____

For Erika Wakerly

First published 2009 by Walker Books Ltd
87 Vauxhall Walk, London SE11 5HJ

This edition published 2010

2 4 6 8 10 9 7 5 3 1

This book has been typeset in Gill Sans MT Schoolbook

Printed in China

British Library Cataloguing in Publication Data:
a catalogue record for this book is available
from the British Library

ISBN 978-1-4063-2615-4

www.walker.co.uk

Tilly and
her friends
all live
together in
a little yellow
house...

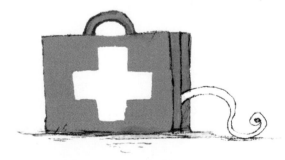

Doodle
Bites

Polly Dunbar

WALKER BOOKS
AND SUBSIDIARIES
LONDON · BOSTON · SYDNEY · AUCKLAND

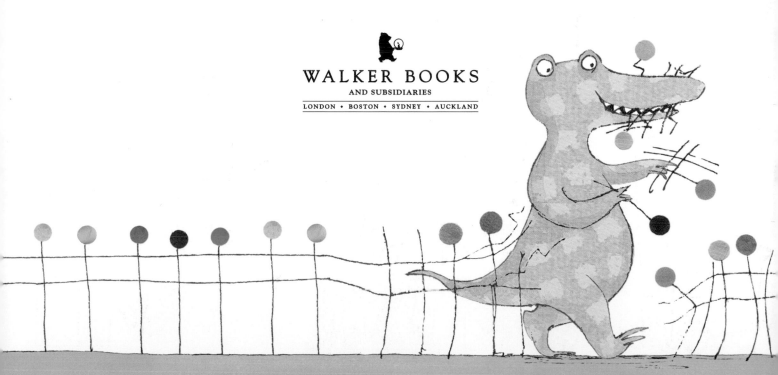

Doodle

woke up

feeling

After she had CHOMPED her breakfast,

she CHEWED the post.

She even CRUNCHED and

MUNCHED the sofa.

While she was NIBBLING the lamp,

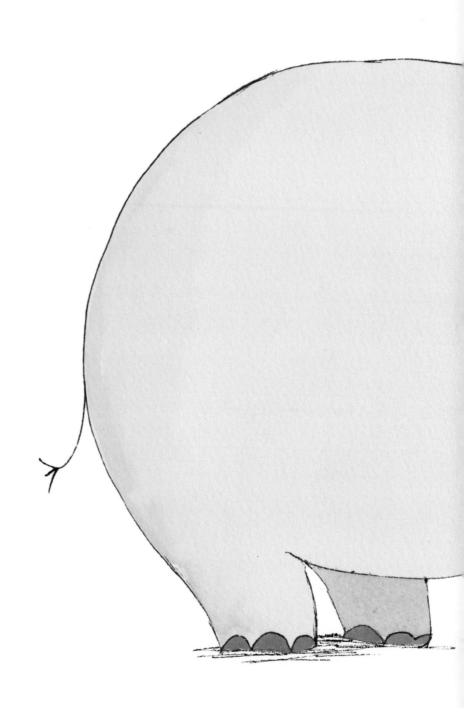

Doodle spied something very good to bite.

"OW!"

shouted Tumpty. "That's my bottom!"

Tumpty was very upset.

"You shouldn't bite
your friends,"
said Tilly.
"It's not
nice."

"Mmm,"
said Doodle.

BITEY! BITEY!

So Tumpty stamped on Doodle's tail.

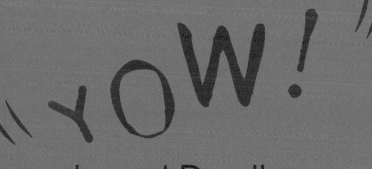

"YOW!"

shouted Doodle.

"That's my tail!"

"You shouldn't
stamp on
your friends,"
said Tilly,
"even if they
bite you.

"It's not nice."

Tumpty was crying.

Doodle was

crying.

Even Hector started crying.

"Don't worry, I'm here!" said Pru,
and she gave Tumpty an
extra-large plaster
for his bottom.

Tilly gave Doodle
a bandage for
her tail.

Hector
and Tiptoe
got plasters too.

Then
Pru kissed
everyone
better.

Even Doodle!

"I'm sorry
I stamped
on your tail,"
said Tumpty.

"I'm sorry
I bit your
bottom,"
said Doodle.

Hurray!

Everyone
was happy
again!

But
Doodle still felt
just a little bit bitey!

"Oh no you don't!"
laughed
Tumpty.

Pru gave Doodle an
extra-special
bandage.

No more bitey bitey!

The End

Polly Dunbar

Polly Dunbar is one of today's most exciting young author-illustrators, her warm and witty books captivating children the world over.

Polly based the Tilly and Friends stories on her own experience of sharing a house with friends. Tilly, Hector, Tumpty, Doodle, Tiptoe and Pru are all very different and they don't always get on. But in the little yellow house, full of love and laughter, no one can be sad or cross for long!

ISBN 978-1-4063-2550-8

ISBN 978-1-4063-2551-5

ISBN 978-1-4063-2614-7

ISBN 978-1-4063-2613-0

ISBN 978-1-4063-2615-4

ISBN 978-1-4063-2616-1

"Nobody can draw anything more instantly loveable than one of Dunbar's characters."
Independent on Sunday

Available from all good bookstores

www.walker.co.uk